Avi.
Finding Providence

6/99

Finding Providence

The Story of Roger Williams

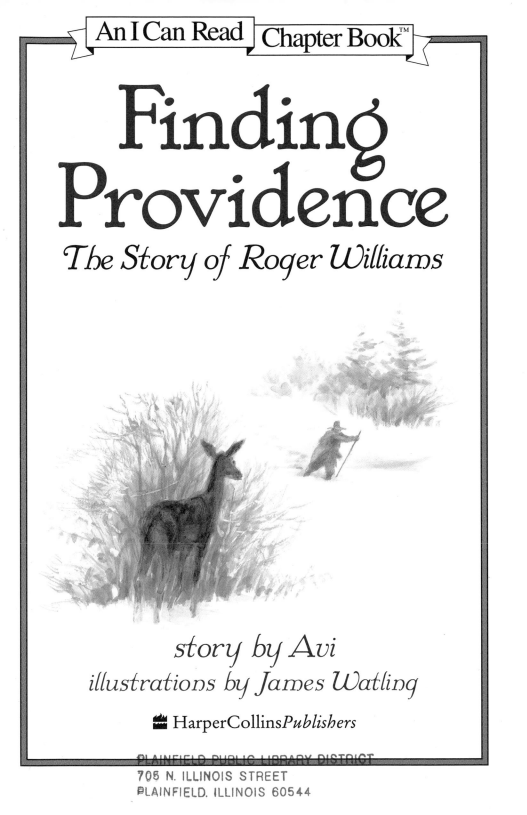

story by Avi

illustrations by James Watling

HarperCollins*Publishers*

To the Children of Providence
—A.

For Jake
—J.W.

HarperCollins®, 📖®, and I Can Read Book® are trademarks of HarperCollins Publishers Inc.

Finding Providence
The Story of Roger Williams
Text copyright © 1997 by Avi
Illustrations copyright © 1997 by James Watling
Printed in the U.S.A. All rights reserved.

Library of Congress Cataloging-in-Publication Data
Avi, date
   Finding Providence : the story of Roger Williams / story by Avi ; pictures by James
Watling.
        p.   cm. — (An I can read chapter book)
   Summary: After being forced to leave the Massachusetts Bay Colony, Roger Williams
travels south and, with the help of the Narragansett Indians, founds Providence, Rhode Island.
   ISBN 0-06-025179-4 — ISBN 0-06-025294-4 (lib. bdg.)
   1. Williams, Roger, 1604?–1683—Juvenile literature.   2. Puritans—Rhode Island—
Biography—Juvenile literature.   3. Baptists—Rhode Island—Biography—Juvenile
literature.   4. Separatists—Rhode Island—Biography—Juvenile literature.   5. Pioneers—
Rhode Island—Biography—Juvenile literature.   6. Rhode Island—Church history—17th
century—Juvenile literature.   [1. Williams, Roger, 1604–1683.   2. United States—
History—Colonial period, ca. 1600–1775—Biography.   3. Reformers.]   I. Watling,
James, ill.   II. Title.
F82.W7A95   1997   95-46360
974.5'02'092—dc20   CIP
[B]   AC

3   4   5   6   7   8   9   10
❖

Contents

1 - The Trial

It was 1635. Inside the General Court of the Massachusetts Bay Colony all was dim and hushed. Judges and ministers sat together at a long table at the front of the room. Standing before these men was my father, Roger Williams.

My mother and I were at the back of the room. My father turned to us and smiled. I squeezed my mother's hand.

The chief minister of Boston, John Cotton, sat in the center of the judges and ministers. "Roger Williams," he said, "you are accused of preaching dangerous new ideas. Will you tell the Court whether or not you truly believe these things?"

Everyone leaned forward. "I have no fear of speaking my mind," said my father.

"Roger Williams," John Cotton said, "do you believe that people should be required to join the church?"

"No," said my father, "not if it is against their wishes."

There was a gasp from the spectators in the court.

"Silence!" cried John Cotton.

"Is it true," said John Cotton, "that you believe that church and government should be separate in all things?"

"Yes. It is wrong for government and church leaders to sit together and tell people how to think and act," said my father.

"How dare he!" a man cried. "What kind of Christian is he?"

"Be quiet!" John Cotton ordered. The soldiers thumped their pikes. The court-room became still.

"And do you believe," said John Cotton, "that we Europeans have no right to take the Indians' land?"

"Impossible!" called out one of the spectators.

"What say you to this last charge, Roger Williams?" asked John Cotton.

My father spoke carefully. "I have come to know the Indians well. They are humans just as we are. They cannot take the King of England's land. We have no right to take theirs."

"Traitor!" one of the spectators cried, and hissed. The judges frowned.

John Cotton shook his head sadly. "Roger Williams," he said, "go home and await our verdict."

I stood up to see my father's face. My mother pulled me down, but I saw he was not smiling.

2 - Danger

Thump, thump, thump!

The banging on our door woke me. For anyone to come at such a time meant something important. I peered out through the small window and saw a man. A lantern was in his hand.

The man knocked again, louder than before. *Thump! Thump! Thump!*

I gathered my blanket around me and crept to the top of the steps. My father went to the door. He did not see me. I sat on the shadowy steps to watch and listen.

"Who's there?" my father called. He tried to keep his voice low. He did not want to wake anyone in the house, but my mother had already gotten up.

14

"Roger Williams?" called the man from outside. "Are you there? It is I, Goodman Neal. I bring grave news!"

My father looked around to my mother. "It's a friend," he said, and drew back the bolts of the door.

Once inside, Goodman Neal brushed the snow from his shoulders and stamped his cold feet on the floor.

"What brings you at such an hour, friend?" my father asked.

"It's what we feared," said Goodman Neal. He kept his voice low. "They are coming to send you away."

"Who is coming?"

"John Cotton and the others," Goodman Neal said. "You have been judged guilty. You are to be sent back to England."

"England!" my mother cried.

"Aye."

"In England the King will put Roger in prison," my mother said. "Or even hang him for his preaching."

"Goodwife Williams, our own leaders would do the same."

18

"I only want every person to think for himself," my father said.

"Even so, sir," Goodman Neal said, "John Cotton is chief minister, and his friends will not allow you to preach your ideas here."

"Goodman Neal," my mother said, "do you know when they are coming?"

"I fear you will see them before dawn. They are sending Captain Gillmore."

"But he is supposed to sail to England tomorrow," said my father.

"Exactly," replied Goodman Neal. "The captain will have soldiers with him to force you onto his ship. They plan to sail by the morning's tide."

"You can't go to other towns, Roger," my
mother said. "You must leave Massachusetts.
Your enemies are everywhere."

"It is so, Mr. Williams," agreed
Goodman Neal. "It is that or a winter's
voyage to an unfriendly England."

My father stood still. "And to think," he said sadly, "just a few years ago we came to New England to gain our religious liberty." He turned to Goodman Neal and held out his hand. "I thank you for your kindness, sir."

"Nay, sir, do not thank me. I do not always agree with all you say, but it's cruel to punish a man for his thoughts. I wish you Godspeed." With a nod to my mother Goodman Neal hurried away.

When he had gone, my mother said, "Will you go, Roger?"

"I must," he said.

"But where?" I cried out from the steps.

My father looked around and was surprised to see me. "Mary," he said, "have you been listening?"

"Where will you go?" I asked again.

"They gave me no choice," he said. "I shall travel into the wilderness."

3 ~ The Escape

My father dressed in his warmest clothing, boots, double linen, and cloak. He took bread and dried meat in a sack. Then he fetched a long stick from the pile of firewood.

"What is that stick for?" I asked. "Are you going to fight the bears?"

"Nay, child. It will help me get through the snow."

"But what about the Indians? Aren't you scared of them?"

"Remember, Mary, that I know the Narragansett Indians' language and their ways. We are friends."

When my father was ready to go, he hugged me, my baby brother, and my mother.

I began to cry. My father wiped the tears from my face. "Put your faith in God," he told me. "He will care. That care, Mary, is what we call God's providence. I shall surely find it."

I watched him from our little window as long as I could. Soon he was lost in the snowy white darkness.

I rushed to my mother and buried my face in her lap.

"We must do as your father bid," she whispered sadly. "Trust in His providence."

At dawn Captain Gillmore and four soldiers came to arrest my father. They were too late. He was long gone.

"Oh, Father," I whispered to myself again and again. "Find God's providence."

4 - The Wilderness

Later my father told me how he walked south into the forests through great drifts of snow. There were no roads and he did not know the Indian trails. There were no inns or houses where he could stay along the way.

At first his only plan was to get away
from the Bay Colony. But as he slowly
made his way south, he tried to find his
friends the Narragansetts.

Again and again he lost his way. Again
and again he had to take his bearings from
the position of the sun and the stars. When
storms came, he found shelter in the hollows
of trees or in caves.

Soon he ran out of food, but he recalled some of the things his Indian friends had taught him about finding food in the forest. He searched and found dried berries, nuts, and other things to eat. It was just enough to allow him to move on.

The farther he went, the weaker he became. As he continued to walk south, he prayed long and hard for strength.

One night, as he fell asleep in the hollow of a tree, he wondered if he would ever see a living person again.

5 - Finding Providence

It was dawn when a touch woke my father. Startled, he looked out from the tree trunk. Standing before him was a Narragansett hunter.

"I am Roger Williams," my father said in the Narragansett language. "I am lost and have no food. Please help me."

The hunter smiled. "Roger Williams, we know you for a friend. Follow me and I will lead you to our village."

The Narragansetts welcomed my father and invited him to live with them. He did so for fourteen weeks.

While he was there, he and the leaders
of the Narragansetts spent many hours
talking about religion and government.

"You and your family may live among
us," they told him. "You have learned our
language and begun to know us. We trust
you to live in peace."

The Indians offered my father a place outside the Bay Colony at the head of beautiful Narragansett Bay. It had a rich spring of sweet water.

My father was overjoyed. He decided to build a new home for us right there. Since it was not safe for him to go back to Boston, an Indian friend carried the message to us.

I saw the Indian come to our house. He greeted me with a smile and handed me a letter. I could see it was written in my father's hand. I ran to my mother. She read the letter out loud.

"Come with my friend and join me," my father had written. "We have been given a new place to live. We can be free here."

We packed hastily and made our way south. In time other families joined us to form a new settlement.

As my father and I stood on the bluff overlooking the bay and the tiny settlement, I felt proud of him.

"Father," I said, "don't you think we should give the village a name?"

"We should," he agreed. "And what do you think it should be called?"

I thought for a moment. Then I said, "Call it Providence. Because of God's providence to you in your distress."

He smiled. "A good name. Providence it shall be. And may it continue to be the freest place on earth."

Author's Note

Roger Williams was born in 1603 or 1604 in London, England. At that time the English church and government were closely intertwined. The king was the head of the church, and he and Parliament made laws that required people to practice religion in certain ways. To be opposed to this way of life was to be a "dissenter."

Roger Williams and his wife came to America in 1631 to be among dissenters who called themselves Puritans because they wished to "purify" the English church. But in Massachusetts the Puritan church soon became almost as inflexible as the old English church.

What makes Williams special is that, while he was a devout Christian, he believed it was wrong for any church or government to force religious beliefs on anyone. When Williams established Providence in 1636, it was to create a place where the separation of church and state could become a way of life. Due in part to Roger Williams's heroic struggles so long ago, this separation is now established in the United States Constitution.